Where's my sock?

First published in 2009
by Wayland

This paperback edition published in 2010

Text copyright © Anne Rooney 2009
Illustration copyright © Fabiano Fiorin 2009

Wayland
338 Euston Road
London NW1 3BH

Wayland Australia
Level 17/207 Kent Street
Sydney, NSW 2000

Series Editor: Louise John
Editor: Katie Powell
Cover design: Paul Cherrill
Design: D.R.ink
Consultant: Shirley Bickler

A CIP catalogue record for this book is available from the British Library.

ISBN 9780750255455 (hbk)
ISBN 9780750255493 (pbk)

Printed in China

Wayland is a division of Hachette Children's Books,
an Hachette Livre UK Company

www.hachettelivre.co.uk

where's my sock?

vidara

Adme

Written by Anne Rooney
Illustrated by Fabiano Fiorin

WAYLAND

"Henry, are you ready
for school?" called Dad.
Kate was waiting by the
door with her coat on.

Henry didn't have his coat on. Henry's jumper was on back to front.

He had jam on his face
and he was only wearing
one sock.

Mum turned Henry's jumper round.

Dad wiped Henry's hands
and his face.

But his sock was still missing.

Henry wiggled his toes.
"I've lost my sock," he said.
"I can't go to school with one
sock on!"

"Quick! Everyone look for
Henry's sock," said Mum.

Mum found a black woolly sock in the clothes basket. It was much too big for Henry.

"So that's where my sock is!"
said Dad.

Dad found a dirty grey sock behind the bathroom door. There was a spider hiding in it!

"I don't know whose sock that is," Mum said. "I've never seen it before."

Henry found a smelly orange sock in Axel's basket. Axel had chewed a hole in it.

No one wanted to touch
that sock.

"You can wear one of my socks," said Kate. She went upstairs to get one.

Kate held the sock out
to Henry.

"I can't wear that!" Henry said. "It's pink and it's got a FAIRY on it!"

"Time to go," Dad called.
"Come on, Henry," shouted
Kate. "We'll be late!"

Henry was getting cross. He
didn't want to wear Kate's
pink fairy sock.

"I am NOT wearing that sock," said Henry.

"Fine," said Mum. "Then your foot will just have to get cold."

At school, Henry met his friend Raheem.

"Hello, Henry!" said Raheem. "We went shopping on Saturday and I bought you a present."

Henry tore the shiny red
paper off the present.
It was a pair of green
dinosaur socks!

No holes. No spiders.
No soggy bits. No pink and,
best of all, NO FAIRIES!

"Perfect!" cried Henry. "This is the best present ever!"

"Look! I've got a matching pair!" laughed Raheem.

START READING is a series of highly enjoyable books for beginner readers. **The books have been carefully graded to match the Book Bands widely used in schools.** This enables readers to be sure they choose books that match their own reading ability.

Look out for the Band colour on the book in our Start Reading logo.

The Bands are:

Pink Band 1

Red Band 2

Yellow Band 3

Blue Band 4

Green Band 5

Orange Band 6

Turquoise Band 7

Purple Band 8

Gold Band 9

START READING books can be read independently or shared with an adult. They promote the enjoyment of reading through satisfying stories supported by fun illustrations.

Anne Rooney has many socks, but none with dinosaurs on. She lives in a state of chaos with her two daughters, a tortoise called Tor2 and a blue lobster called Marcel.

Fabiano Fiorin lives and works in a magical city, Venice, where there are canals full of sea water instead of roads, and there are boats instead of cars. Fabiano thinks the best thing about being an illustrator is that you can pretend to be the characters you draw and you can have lots of adventures.